FINS AND SCALES

A KOSHER TALE

Deborah Uchill Miller and Karen Ostrove

illustrated by Karen Ostrove

KAR-BEN COPIES, INC.   ROCKVILLE, MD

Library of Congress Cataloging-in-Publication Data

Miller, Deborah
    Fins and scales: a kosher tale/Deborah Uchill Miller and Karen Ostrove: illustrated by
Karen Ostrove.
      p.   cm.
    Summary: The Jewish dietary laws of keeping kosher are explained in humorous
rhyme.
    ISBN 0-929371-25-9:   — ISBN 0-929371-26-7 (pbk.):
    [1. Jews—Dietary laws—Fiction. 2. Kosher food—Fiction. 3. Food habits— Fic-
tion. 4. Stories in rhyme.] I. Ostrove, Karen. ill. II. Title.
    PZ8.3.M61325F1 1991
    [E]—dc20   90-24388
                                                        CIP
                                                        AC

This book is dedicated
to those that made it all possible - our parents!
Ida and Sam Uchill
Sophie (z''l) and Robert Davis
... and, of course, Grandma Kate

"Teach your children in the way you want them to grow..." (Proverbs)

In memory of our friend
Barbara S. Shaw (z''l)
She laughed in all the right places.

When Yoni Katz was turning eight,
He got a check from Grandma Kate.

She wrote, "Buy something just for you—
A kite, a comic, or kazoo."

So many things to choose, thought Yoni.
Maybe I should get a pony.

"Dad, please help me pick a treat.
Which of these is really neat?"

His folks were in an eating mood
And therefore only thought of food.

So Mom said, "Pick what you like best,
But it must pass the kosher test."

"Kosher?!! Please explain to me
Just what a kosher gift can be."

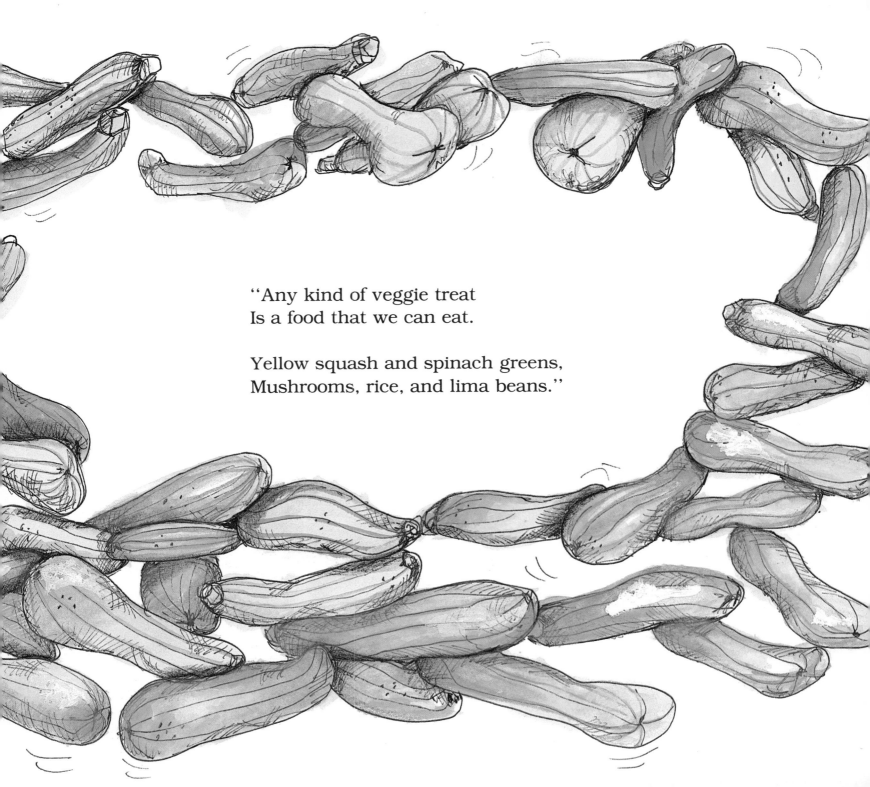

"Any kind of veggie treat
Is a food that we can eat.

Yellow squash and spinach greens,
Mushrooms, rice, and lima beans."

"Just a minute, Mom," said Yoni.
"I'm not into minestrone.

I need help in picking out
A treat that's not a Brussels sprout.''

"Eat an apple with the peel,
But not a shark and not an eel."

"Have some kasha made from groats
Or muffins baked with wheat or oats."

"Buy bananas by the load,
But not a frog and not a toad.

Eat potatoes long like blimps—
Not the lobsters, not the shrimps."

"Don't eat bears, or snakes that creep.
Our meat can come from cows and sheep.

Their hooves are split, they chew their cud,
Not like pigs that play in mud."

"But what about the fish we eat?
Where are their cuds? Where are their feet?"

"We look for fins and check for scales.
That is why we eat no whales."

"We may eat duck, we may eat goose,
A tall giraffe, a knock-kneed moose.

Never eat a slug or louse,
No mongoose, cat, or furry mouse.

Eat no eagle! Eat no gnat!
And never serve souffle of bat!"

"Dad, I think I understand
What's kosher on the sea and land.

But the gift I have in mind
Is really of another kind."

"Don't mix foods of milk and meat.
A cheeseburger's no kosher treat.

And after eating meat we wait
Before there's dairy on our plate."

"Special marks on food in boxes
Tell us if our cheese or lox is
Kosher. So, please check your snacks
For symbols printed on the packs.

These signs mean someone did decide
There's only kosher food inside."

"Thank you both for teaching me
The kosher rules so thoroughly.

I now know all about the meat
And fish and greens and fowl we eat.

But I've been thinking this thing through,
And have a thought to share with you,

It's nothing that a check can buy,
It's not some food you steam or fry.

I've decided Dad and Mother,
My gift should be...

A BABY BROTHER!"

About Keeping Kosher ⟶

KEEPING KOSHER

Why do people keep kosher?

Among the reasons some people keep kosher are:

- Keeping kosher is a *mitzvah* (commandment) in the Torah.
- Keeping kosher helps develop a sensitivity to animals and life.
- Keeping kosher strengthens Jewish identity and carries on Jewish traditions.
- Keeping kosher adds an element of holiness to the everyday activity of eating.

What foods are kosher?

- Fruits and vegetables, nuts and grains, milk products in their natural state.
- The meat of animals that chew their cud *and* have split hooves (examples are cows, sheep, goats); and certain birds (chicken, ducks, turkeys, geese). However, these animals and birds must be slaughtered according to Jewish law and soaked and salted to remove all blood.
- Fish are kosher if they have fins and scales.
- Packaged and processed food - from soup to nuts - is kosher if it has a symbol *(hechsher)* that certifies that all the ingredients are kosher and preparation was supervised.

What foods may be eaten together?

People who keep kosher may not eat milk and meat products at the same meal, or cook them together. They have separate dishes, pots and pans, and silverware for meat meals and dairy meals.

Parve foods (vegetables, fruit, grains, fish, nuts and oils) may be eaten with either milk or meat meals.

* * *

There are special rules for keeping kosher on Passover.

* * *

Your rabbi is the best source for specific information on keeping kosher.

ABOUT THE AUTHORS

Debby Miller is the director of the Solomon Schechter Day School of the Raritan Valley in East Brunswick, NJ. A Denver native, she is a graduate of Barnard College and the Jewish Theological Seminary. Debby is married to Rabbi Clifford Miller, and they have two daughters, Arielle and Adinah.

Karen Ostrove, cartoonist, ventriloquist and inveterate doodler, has illustrated books, greeting cards, and numerous magazine articles. She created "T'kiah the Rambunctious One," a cartoon feature of *Shofar* magazine. Karen was born and raised in the metropolitan New York area and now lives with husband Steven and children Elliot, Philip, and Naomi in Elizabeth, NJ.

Debby and Karen have collaborated previously on *Only Nine Chairs*, now a Passover classic, *Poppy Seeds, Too*, a twisted tale of challah-baking and *Modi'in Motel*, an "idol" tale about Hanukkah, all published by Kar-Ben Copies. Their popular storytelling performances have become favorite entertainment at Jewish bookfairs around the country.